W9-ATB-036

EMMA
Every Day

Swimming Struggle

by C.L. Reid

illustrated by Elena Aiello

PICTURE WINDOW BOOKS

a capstone imprint

Published by Picture Window Books, an imprint of Capstone
1710 Roe Crest Drive, North Mankato, Minnesota 56003
capstonepub.com

Copyright © 2023 by Capstone
All rights reserved. No part of this publication may be reproduced
in whole or in part, or stored in a retrieval system, or transmitted
in any form or by any means, electronic, mechanical, photocopying,
recording, or otherwise, without written permission of the publisher.

Library of Congress Cataloging-in-Publication Data
Names: Reid, C. L., author. | Aiello, Elena (Illustrator), illustrator.
Title: Swimming struggle / by C. L. Reid ; illustrated by Elena Aiello.
Description: North Mankato, Minnesota : Picture Window Books, [2023]
| Series: Emma every day | Audience: Ages 5-7. | Audience: Grades K-1.
| Summary: After Emma makes the swim team her best friend, Izzie,
(who did not make it) has started to avoid her, and Emma fears that
she will have to choose between the swim team and her friendship.
Identifiers: LCCN 2021970047 (print) | LCCN 2021058787 (ebook) | ISBN
9781666338706 (hardcover) | ISBN 9781666338720 (paperback) | ISBN
9781666338713 (pdf) | ISBN 9781666338744 (kindle edition)
Subjects: LCSH: Deaf children—Juvenile fiction. | Swim teams—Juvenile
fiction. | Best friends—Juvenile fiction. | Choice (Psychology)—Juvenile
fiction. | CYAC: Deaf—Fiction. | Swimming—Fiction. | Best friends—Fiction. |
Friendship—Fiction. | Choice (Psychology)—Fiction. | LCGFT:
Picture books. Classification: LCC PZ7.1.R4544 Sw 2022 (print) |
LCC PZ7.1.R4544 (ebook) | DDC 813.6 [E]—dc23/eng/20211215
LC record available at https://lccn.loc.gov/2021970047
LC ebook record available at https://lccn.loc.gov/2021970109

Image Credits: Capstone: Daniel Griffo, top right 28, bottom 29, Mick Reid,
bottom left 28, bottom right 28, Randy Chewning, top left 28

Design elements: Shutterstock: achii, Maric C, Mika Besfamilnaya

Special thanks to Evelyn Keolian for her consulting work.

Editor's note: Throughout the book, a few words are called out and
fingerspelled using ASL. Some of these words have ASL signs too.

Designer: Nathan Gassman

Printed and bound in the USA. 4882

TABLE OF CONTENTS

MEET EMMA

EMMA CARTER
Age: 8 Grade: 3

SIBLING
one brother, Jaden
(12 years old)

PARENTS
David and Lucy

BEST FRIEND
Izzie Jackson

PET
a goldfish named Ruby

favorite color: teal
favorite food: tacos
favorite school subject: writing
favorite sport: swimming
hobbies: reading, writing, biking, swimming

FINGERSPELLING GUIDE

MANUAL ALPHABET

Aa   Bb   Cc   Dd   Ee

Ff   Gg   Hh   Ii   Jj

MANUAL NUMBERS

0   1   2   3

Emma is Deaf. She uses American Sign Language (ASL) to communicate with her family. She also uses a cochlear implant (CI) to help her hear some sounds.

Kk   Ll   Mm   Nn   Oo

Pp   Qq   Rr   Ss   Tt   Uu

Vv   Ww   Xx   Yy   Zz

4   5   6   7   8   9   10

Chapter 1
Tryouts

Emma and her best friend, Izzie, just finished trying out for the Flippers  swim team. Emma dried her hair and put on her Cochlear Implant (CI).

"I hope we made the team,"
Emma signed to Izzie.

"Me too," Izzie signed. "It would
be fun to do it together."

"Come on! Let's go to the
lobby.  Coach is going
to announce the team," Emma signed.

Phhheeew! A whistle blew. The room grew quiet.

"Great job, everyone!" Coach Jones said. "I would like to make everyone members of the swim team, but we only have eight spots."

She held up a paper. "Here

is this year's team. Emma Carter!"

called the coach.

Everyone cheered. Emma smiled.

The coach called seven more names, but Izzie wasn't one of them. Emma's smile disappeared.

"Practice starts tomorrow," Coach said.

Emma and Izzie looked at each other. Emma wasn't excited about making the swim team anymore.

"You should go on and join the team," Izzie signed. She tried to smile.

But Emma knew Izzie was disappointed. Should she still join the team? Would Izzie still be her best friend?

Chapter 2
Alone

On Monday, Emma waited for Izzie at the corner. That's where they always met to walk to school. But after ten minutes, Emma guessed Izzie was sick. She hurried to school by herself.

The next day at school, Emma saw Izzie in the hall.

But Izzie didn't stop to talk with her.

Emma thought Izzie was busy.

Wednesday at recess,  Izzie played basketball with other kids. Emma figured Izzie had become interested in basketball.

But on Thursday at lunchtime,
Izzie sat with a different group of
kids. Emma sat alone.

Why was Izzie avoiding
her? Emma felt lonely, sad, and
confused. She missed Izzie.

That night before Emma got into

bed, she talked to her goldfish.

"Ruby, 🤟 should I quit

the team? It could be so much fun.

But I also don't want to lose Izzie's

friendship."

Ruby kept swimming in circles. Emma took off her CI and crawled into bed. She tossed and turned all night. What should she do?

Chapter 3

Friends Forever

Emma didn't want to go to

school on Friday. She missed her

friend. She didn't even want to

swim anymore.

Her morning dragged along. By
lunchtime, Emma was miserable.
She grabbed her food and went
to her table.

Once again, she sat alone.

Just then, Izzie walked over to Emma's table.

"Can I sit with you?" she signed.

"Of course," Emma signed.

They both ate in silence. It was awful. Then Izzie took a deep breath and spoke up.

"I am sorry, Emma," Izzie signed.
"I was sad and jealous. I really
wanted to make the team too."

Emma's face brightened with a smile. "I forgive you. I am going to quit the team."

"Don't do that! I am happy that you made the team," Izzie signed.

"But I want us to be friends," Emma signed.

"We will be friends forever," Izzie sighed. "And I will come cheer  you on."

They did their secret handshake and laughed.

On Saturday, Emma had her first swim meet. She was nervous. Her parents and brother were there. Izzie was there too.

Before Emma's race, Izzie waved and cheered. Then she held up a sign she had made for Emma.

All of Emma's nerves melted. She

was ready to race!

LEARN TO SIGN

fish

Hold hand sideways
and wiggle.

sad

Move hands down
in front of face.

swimming

Move hands in small circles.

water

Make W shape and tap
mouth twice.

swimsuit

1. Move hands in small circles.
2. Slide hands along chest and waist.

friend

1. Lock fingers.
2. Repeat with other hand on top.

GLOSSARY

avoid—to ignore

Cochlear Implant (also called CI)—a device that helps someone who is Deaf to hear; it is worn on the head just above the ear

deaf—being unable to hear

fingerspell—to make letters with your hands to spell out words; often used for names of people and places

jealous—wanting something someone else has

sign language—a language in which hand gestures, along with facial expressions and body movements, are used to communicate

TALK ABOUT IT

1. Do you think Izzie was being a good friend to Emma?

2. The author writes that Emma's heart felt heavy. What does that mean?

3 . What would you do if you didn't make a team you tried out for?

WRITE ABOUT IT

1. Make a list of things you would like to try out for.

2. Pretend you are Izzie. Write an apology note to Emma.

3. Write about a time you felt disappointed.

ABOUT THE AUTHOR

Deaf-blind since childhood, C.L. Reid received a cochlear implant (CI) as an adult to help her hear, and she uses American Sign Language (ASL) to communicate. She and her husband have three sons. Their middle son is also deaf-blind. C.L. earned a master's degree in writing for children and young adults at Hamline University in St. Paul, Minnesota. She lives in Minnesota with her husband, two of their sons, and their cats.

ABOUT THE ILLUSTRATOR

Elena Aiello is an illustrator and character designer. After graduating as a marketing specialist, she decided to study art direction and CGI. Doing so, she discovered a passion for illustration and conceptual art. She works as a freelancer for various magazines and publishers. Elena loves video games and sushi. She lives with her husband and her little pug, Gordon, in Milan, Italy.